S0-AWQ-928

BEANIE

The Horse That Wasn't a Horse

Heather Grovet

Pacific Press® Publishing Association
Nampa, Idaho
Oshawa, Ontario, Canada
www.pacificpress.com

Designed by Dennis Ferree
Cover art by Mary Rumford

Copyright © 2004 by
Pacific Press® Publishing Association
Printed in United States of America
All Rights Reserved

Additional copies of this book are available
by calling toll free 1-800-765-6955 or by
visiting http://www.adventistbookcenter.com

ISBN: 0-8163-2053-5

04 05 06 07 08 · 5 4 3 2 1

Contents

Other Books in the Julius and Friends Series

Dedication

To Marjorie.
Mothers are forever.

CHAPTER

1

A Dream Comes True

Nine-year-old Alex Jahns pulled the blankets over his face so that only his short, blond hair showed, and closed his eyes. But even though Alex's eyes were closed, he was not asleep. Instead of being tired, Alex was wide awake. How could he sleep when tomorrow was going to be the most wonderful day of his entire life?

It's like an answer to prayer! Alex thought happily. *I prayed for a horse, and God finally answered my prayer with a "Yes"!*

Alex was horse crazy. His father was horse crazy. Alex's mother was *not* horse crazy. "*Horses* are crazy," Mom liked to joke, "and a person would have to be crazy to like them!"

Alex had read dozens of horse books. He knew every part of *The Black Stallion* and *My Friend Flicka* and *Black Beauty* by heart. But until now Alex's dream of owning a real live horse had seemed impossible.

"With God all things are possible," Alex said out loud. And then he smiled again, remembering Grandpa Stevens' phone call that evening.

"Alex," Grandpa had asked, "would you like a horse of your own?"

"Of course I would," Alex said.

Alex's mother was standing nearby, and she shook her head when she heard Grandpa's question. "We don't have enough money to buy a horse right now," she said. "Unless it's a toy horse—a cheap toy horse."

"What if the horse were free?" Grandpa asked, "would you want it then?"

"A free horse?" Alex's heart began to pound. He'd wanted a horse all his life—

a beautiful horse, an elegant horse, a wonderful horse. Alex shook his head to clear his thoughts and pressed the phone closer to his ear, wondering if he had heard correctly.

Grandpa chuckled. "That's right," he said. "I know where you can get a good horse, free."

"A free horse?" Alex asked again.

"Any free horse probably has only three legs," Dad grumbled when he overheard Alex. "Or two heads."

"Dad!" Alex hissed.

"Or maybe it has three legs *and* two heads!" Dad continued.

"We don't want a two-headed horse," Mom said. "Think how much hay it would eat!"

"I'm sure it doesn't have three legs and two heads," Alex said quickly.

"Alex, I know how much you'd like a horse," Dad said, "but good horses are very expensive. There has to be something wrong with a horse that's free."

Grandpa explained that his friend, Roger Jacobson, had fallen and broken his hip.

The doctors said Roger shouldn't ride his horse anymore. "Roger just wants him to have a good home," Grandpa told the family. "He's a really nice animal, but he needs someone to love and care for him."

"I'll love him!" Alex shouted into the phone. "I'll take care of him! I'll do anything for a horse of my own!"

"Alex," Grandpa laughed, "you don't need to yell. I'm not deaf. Or at least, I wasn't deaf before this!"

"Sorry," Alex said, lowering his voice, "but I'm just so excited, Grandpa! A free horse! For me!"

"You need to come and look at him," Grandpa said.

"What's his name?" Alex asked. Horse names flew through his head—wonderful, elegant, powerful horse names such as *Flame* and *Blaze* and *Thunder* and *Beauty.*

"Beanie," Grandpa replied.

"Beanie?"

"Roger calls him Beanie," Grandpa said. "Although I imagine you could change the name if you wanted."

Alex's mother snorted in the background, sounding a bit like a horse herself. "Beanie!" she exclaimed. "What sort of name is that?"

"Mom!" Alex frowned, covering the phone receiver so Grandpa couldn't hear them. "Be nice."

"Bean Brain is probably more like it," Mom continued.

"Don't make fun of my horse," Alex said. He felt protective of Beanie already, as though the horse were on the other end of the phone line, listening to someone tease him.

"Alex," Grandpa said, "let's meet tomorrow at the Jacobson farm. You need to have a good look at Beanie before making any decisions. After all, owning a horse is a big responsibility."

"Oh, Grandpa," Alex said, "you don't need to worry. I'm very responsible."

Mom cleared her throat. "What about your hamster?" she asked.

"I take good care of Hammie," Alex insisted.

"No, *I* take good care of Hammie,"

Mom said. "And I imagine *I* would have to take good care of your horse, too."

"That's different," Alex said. "You can't ride a hamster. You can't train a hamster. You can't do anything with a hamster."

"I told you that you'd have to be crazy to like hamsters," Mom said. "But you insisted a hamster would be fun. Now we're stuck with one, and it does nothing but sit around and eat all day."

"Mom!"

"And you'd have to be crazy to like horses, too," Mom continued.

"A horse is different from a hamster," Alex said.

"That's for sure," Mom agreed. "A horse smells worse and eats a lot more!"

"Alex," Grandpa asked, "are you still there?"

"I'm here, Grandpa," Alex answered quickly.

"Why don't you three talk about the horse tonight," Grandpa suggested. "I'll phone you back tomorrow, and if you're still interested, we can drive out and look at Beanie in the afternoon. OK?"

"Thank you, Grandpa," Alex said. "Thank you, thank you, thank you!"

"Don't thank me until you see Beanie," Grandpa said. "He's actually a funny looking thing—brown with big white spots—and you might not even want him. But he's very well trained. Roger rode Beanie in the mountains for years, and a few summers ago they even won a bunch of ribbons at the Stettler Gymkhana Races." Alex knew that "gymkhana" races just meant a variety of events for riders and their horses to perform in. They were sponsored by the local riding club in Stettler.

When Alex hung up the phone, he looked at his parents. His father was smiling an enormous smile that almost split his face in two. But Alex's mother didn't look so cheerful. "Of course the horse is a funny-looking thing," Mom said. "I've never seen a horse that wasn't funny looking."

"Mom!"

"They have those great big hooves that can squash your toes, and those long teeth to bite you with, and fuzzy hair that they shed everywhere. I'm certain this horse won't be any different from the rest."

"Don't you want me to have a horse?" Alex asked. "If it's free?"

"Not really," Mom said. "Remember, I hate horses. Besides, I think you're busy tomorrow, Alex. You'll never find the time to look at a horse."

"Busy?"

"Homework," Mom replied. "You're going to be very busy with homework tomorrow."

"It's the summer holidays!"

"That's no excuse," Mom said.

Alex was about to argue when he looked closely at his mother. Her blue eyes were sparkling, and a smile twitched on her lips.

Alex raced over to his parents and threw an arm around each of them. "This is the best day of my life!" he shouted. Then he thought for a moment. "No, tomorrow will be the best day of my life. Because that's the day that I get a horse of my own!"

After Mom had tucked Alex into bed, he lay hidden under the covers, too excited to sleep. A horse of his own! Yes, tomorrow was going to be the most wonderful day of his life. The most wonderful, incredible, amazing day of his life! Alex tossed and turned for a long time before he finally drifted off to sleep. Almost immediately he began to dream.

Alex was riding on the most beautiful horse in the world. It was jet black like the Black Stallion. His coat gleamed in the sunlight, and his thick mane and tail rippled in the wind. Alex was riding the beautiful horse like an expert. They were galloping, free and wild, across a field thick with brilliant yellow flowers. Alex could feel the breeze in his short blond hair and the swaying of each enormous stride. Up and down, up and down, up and down.

Suddenly the dream became weird. The Black Stallion began to change. His jet black hair began to turn a dull white color. The mane and tail disappeared, and the horse became short and chubby and furry.

It was Hammie! Alex was galloping across the field on Hammie, his hamster! And now that he was close to the ground, he could see that the beautiful yellow flowers were nothing more than dandelions.

A hamster and a bunch of weeds. What a horrible way for a perfect dream to end!

CHAPTER

2

Dream or Nightmare?

"Let me introduce you," Grandpa Stevens said with a polite bow. "Alex, this is Beanie, the hinny. And Beanie, this is Alex. He's a nice kid, but he's a bit crazy. Horse crazy, that is."

Alex didn't say anything. He just stared at the white and brown animal standing in front of him. Even horse-crazy Alex had to admit that Beanie was very strange looking. The animal's head was enormous and shaped like a bucket. Two long floppy ears topped the highest corners of the bucket-shaped head. *Rabbit ears,* Alex thought a bit unkindly. *Great big, jack rabbit-ears.*

Beanie's head connected to a short, thick neck thinly decorated by little wisps of white mane. The neck merged into a long, sausage-shaped body. Four short, stubby legs and a scrawny rat tail completed the picture.

Alex knew that Beanie couldn't be a horse—at least he didn't look like any horse Alex had ever seen before. But if Beanie wasn't a horse, what kind of animal was he? Ears like a jack rabbit, a head like an empty bucket, a body like a dachshund dog, short legs like a cow, and a little rat tail made the animal seem like a mixed-up jigsaw puzzle. *With a piece or two missing, maybe,* Alex thought with a faint frown.

"This isn't a horse," Mom said. "It's a donkey! And an ugly one at that."

"Beanie isn't a donkey," Grandpa assured them.

"A mule?" Dad asked.

"Nope."

"Maybe he's a moose," Mom said, "a small moose, without any horns."

"Wrong again," Grandpa said.

"Well, I give up," Mom said. "What is this thing?"

"Weren't you listening?" Grandpa said. "I told you when I introduced Beanie to Alex."

Alex tried to think of what Grandpa had said, but his brain didn't seem to be working that well.

"Beanie is a hinny," Grandpa said proudly.

"A hinny?" Alex asked. "What is a hinny?"

"You're my little hinny, Alex," his mom laughed. "Except you're better looking than Beanie."

"Mom!"

"Your mother's right," Alex's dad said. "Your ears aren't quite as enormous as Beanie's, are they, Alex? And you have nicer legs, too. Not so hairy!"

"I wish everyone would stop picking on Beanie," Grandpa said. "When you get to know him, you'll see he's really very cute."

Mom snickered.

"Now, here's your science lesson for

the day," Grandpa said. "I imagine you've heard of mules before, haven't you?"

Everyone nodded their heads. Even Beanie choose that moment to give his wide head a shake, making it seem that he was listening, too.

"Well," Grandpa continued. "Mules have a *horse* for a mother, and a *donkey* for a father. Hinnies have a *donkey* for a mother, and a *horse* for a father."

"Doesn't that still make him a mule?" Dad asked.

"No, it doesn't," Grandpa said. "Hinnies are much rarer than mules. And they're different from mules in many ways."

"Well, he's *different*, all right," Mom agreed.

"Beanie's head is shaped like a donkey's," Alex said. "And he has long donkey ears."

"And he has a horse-shaped body," Grandpa said, "except his legs are short like a donkey's legs."

"Well, at least with those short, little legs you wouldn't have too far to fall," Mom told Alex. Beanie seemed to realize she was talking about him, because he slowly walked toward her and began to sniff her shirt.

Mom quit grinning and quickly backed up a step. "Scram," she shouted. "I don't like horses!"

"Beanie isn't a horse," Alex said. "He's a hinny."

Beanie blinked his big, brown eyes and followed Mrs. Jahns as she continued walking backward.

"I don't like hinnies, either," Mom said, waving her arms. "So vamoose! Scram! Get!"

Beanie took another step her direction.

Mom darted over to the men and tried to hide behind Grandpa Stevens.

Beanie wasn't bothered by her actions. Instead he seemed to think she was just being friendly in a rather odd way. He moved as close as possible to Grandpa and stretched out his thick neck to reach behind him.

"Somebody call 911!" Mom said weakly. "I need help."

"Beanie says you need love," Alex said. Beanie blinked his big brown eyes and nodded his head in agreement.

"Beanie won't hurt you," Grandpa said. He took his hand and pushed against the hinny's chest until the animal took a step backward. "He just wants to be your friend."

"But I don't want to be his friend!" Mom declared, glaring from behind the men.

"It's too late," Grandpa said. "Once a hinny likes you, you're friends for life."

"Then he'll have a rather short life," Mom said.

"Oh no," Grandpa said. "Mules and hinnies can live to be thirty or forty years old. Beanie will be around for a long time."

"Lucky me!" Mom said sarcastically. Beanie stretched his neck further forward and sniffed again.

"He sure likes you, Mom," Alex said.

"Are you carrying oats?" Dad asked, "or other horse treats?"

"Me? Never!"

"Maybe Mom washed her hair with that new apple shampoo!" Alex laughed.

Mom didn't laugh. Instead she reached up and flipped her hair behind her back.

"I don't think she smells like apples," Grandpa said. "I think she smells like Beanie's mother."

"What!" shouted Mom. "I smell like a horse's mother?"

"Beanie's a hinny," Alex said. "Not a horse."

"I'm not a hinny's mother, either," Mom said sharply.

"No," Grandpa said, "but you're a lady. And it was a lady—Mrs. Jacobson—who raised Beanie on a bottle."

"Then tell that beast that I don't have a baby bottle with me!" Mom said. "It's been quite a few years since Alex needed a bottle." She glared at Beanie. Beanie gazed back at her with a love-sick expression on his face.

"Roger's wife *had* to feed Beanie from a bottle," Grandpa continued. "They bought him at a horse auction when he was only a few days old. He was only half alive—just a bag of bones, actually. They were told that Beanie's father was a brown quarter horse stallion, and his mother was a little, white burro. No one really knew what happened to Beanie's mother or how he came to be at the horse auction."

"Well," Dad said, looking at Beanie's fat belly, "they must have done something right, because he certainly isn't a bag of bones anymore!"

"No, he isn't," Grandpa agreed. "And although an orphan baby is an enormous amount of work, it paid off by making Beanie a very special animal. He likes people more than he likes horses. In fact, sometimes Beanie seems to think he is a person himself!"

Beanie slowly moved a step closer to Mrs. Jahns, but this time he didn't try to touch her. Instead he lowered his head and closed his eyes as though he was ready to take a nap near his new friend.

Mom studied the animal carefully. When Beanie didn't move for a few minutes, she finally spoke. "Are you certain he won't bite?" she asked.

"I guarantee it," Grandpa said.

"But does Beanie guarantee it?" Mom asked. Finally she reached out one finger and slowly touched Beanie's neck. Beanie's eyelids fluttered, but he didn't move. Mom's finger shifted up the hinny's neck to his face. She stroked his cheek and then moved to the long, floppy ears. Beanie stood quietly as she began to pet him with increasing courage.

Beanie sighed happily. Mr. Jahns looked at his wife and smiled. Mrs. Jahns returned the smile. "You know, he *is* rather cute," she slowly admitted.

"Cute!" Alex exclaimed.

"He's so ugly he's cute," Mom said.

Alex didn't see anything cute about Beanie. He had read *Black Beauty*. He had read *Misty* and *Thunderhead* and hundreds of other horse books. And none of them had been about a bucket-headed, long-eared hinny. Beanie wasn't the horse for him.

Alex looked at the three adults and frowned. They were all beaming at the little animal as though he were a prize-winning show horse.

Which he definitely wasn't.

"He's as friendly as a big puppy," Mom said. She scratched the floppy ears again. Beanie whisked his thin tail at a fly, causing her to jump for a moment, but when he stood quietly, she began to scratch him again.

"That's why I thought of Alex when Roger said Beanie needed a new home," Grandpa said. "Alex could really learn to ride with an animal as gentle as Beanie."

Alex pressed his lips together. "I already know how to ride," he said quickly.

"Yes," Grandpa said. "I know you took horsemanship at Foothills Camp."

"Advanced horsemanship," Alex corrected.

"Advanced horsemanship," Grandpa nodded. "But there are a lot of things you still can't do, Alex."

"Like what?"

"Like saddle a horse properly," Grandpa said.

"I can saddle a horse," Alex said. "And I can bridle one, too."

"Don't you want Beanie?" Dad asked, turning a puzzled face to Alex.

Alex stiffened his back. He wanted a horse of his own. But did he want Beanie? Never!

Alex had been praying for a horse—not for a hinny. Alex wondered for a moment if this were God's idea of a joke. Everyone would laugh at Beanie. They'd laugh at Alex, too!

But before Alex could answer, Dad answered for him. "Well," he said, "let's see Beanie work before we make up our minds."

Grandpa passed Alex the lead rope before Alex had time to say anything. "Here," he said. "I'll get the saddle and bridle, and we'll see how you manage."

Mom stopped petting Beanie. Slowly Beanie opened his big brown eyes. He sniffed once and then turned to look at Alex. The hinny studied Alex and then nudged his hand with his soft muzzle.

Okay, Beanie seemed to be saying. *Now it's your turn to pet me.*

Alex touched Beanie's nose. The hair on the hinny's face was soft and silky— almost like velvet—and Alex smiled in spite of himself. There was something special about being around a horse, even if it was an especially ugly one.

Grandpa was puffing when he came out of the barn carrying a large western saddle and bridle. He passed Alex the saddle blanket and watched carefully as the boy set it on the hinny's back. Alex managed to saddle Beanie without too many problems, but when Grandpa put the bridle in Alex's hands, Alex hesitated.

"Do I have to put my fingers in Beanie's mouth?" Alex asked nervously. *Those big teeth look like they could easily chomp off a finger or two!* he thought.

Grandpa seemed to know what Alex was thinking, because he winked before picking up the bridle. "Roger named him Beanie because he's brown with white patches," Grandpa said "exactly the same color as a pinto bean."

"And here I thought he was named Beanie because of his awful smell!" Alex's father laughed, pinching his nose.

"Beanie doesn't smell bad," Mom said. "Do you, Beanie Boy?"

Grandpa laughed. Beanie didn't seem the least bit disturbed by Dad's comments. Instead he slowly ambled over to Grandpa and put his big head over the man's shoulder. "Now," Grandpa said to Alex, "you hold the bridle like this, and you put the bit here, and then you . . ."

Grandpa's old, wrinkled hands moved easily, slipping the bridle on and off several times. "Beanie's very well trained," he said. "See how he opens his mouth for me?" Beanie's soft eyes sparkled as he opened his mouth, showing a row of enormous, yellow teeth.

"Someone should brush that poor horse's teeth," Mom said, staring in amazement.

"Horse's teeth are yellow because they eat grass all day," Grandpa said. "But they seldom get cavities. I suppose it's because they don't eat sugar and junk food like some people do."

"Sounds like Beanie's smarter than someone I know," Mom said. Alex pretended he didn't hear the comment and watched carefully as Grandpa did up the bridle's last buckle.

Finally Beanie was properly saddled and bridled.

"Are you ready to hop on?" Grandpa asked, looking at Alex.

"Are you certain it's safe?" Mom asked, looking first at Alex and then at the hinny. "We don't even own a riding helmet."

"Well," Grandpa said, "you should buy Alex a helmet as soon as possible. But I don't think you have to worry about Beanie bucking Alex off. Why, last year Roger stood on Beanie's back when he trimmed the tall branches off his trees."

"So what?" Dad asked. "Anyone could stand on that wide back."

"Even if they were seventy years old?" Grandpa asked.

Dad nodded his head.

"And with a chain saw running?"

Dad blinked. "With a . . . ? "

"Beanie isn't scared very easily," Grandpa said. "Not that I'm suggesting you try using a chain saw while standing on Beanie's back, Alex!"

"Alex with a chain saw!" Mom said. "Alex can barely manage scissors! Why, he'd saw off Beanie's ears before he cut any branches!"

Alex laughed. "Don't worry, Mom," he said. "I won't be using any chain saws this week. Especially while standing on a horse's back!"

"Good," Mom said, "because I'm starting to like those great big ears. We wouldn't want them hurt, now would we, Beanie Boy?"

Alex sighed loudly. His horse-hating mother was becoming a big mush ball right in front of his eyes. And she was falling for the world's ugliest horse!

"Come on, Alex," Grandpa said. "We don't have all day." Alex gave a final frown and grabbed the saddle horn. With a big push, he managed to get himself up into the saddle. Then he awkwardly gathered the reins and began to ride Beanie around the yard.

No, they didn't gallop through the field like Alex did on the black horse in his dream. And the wind didn't blow in Alex's hair and ripple the horse's flowing mane. But Alex had to admit to himself that it felt good to be on a horse.

Even if the *horse* was only a funny-looking *hinny* like Beanie!

CHAPTER

3

A Truck-Riding Hinny

"Eat your toast," Mom ordered, pouring Alex a glass of cold orange juice. "Grandpa will be here with Beanie in a few minutes."

Alex pushed his toast around the plate gloomily. "I'm not hungry," he said.

"Quick, everyone," Dad said. "Mark this day on the calendar! It's the first time I've ever known Alex to be full!"

Alex sighed. "I don't want any juice either, Mom," he said.

"How about some raspberry yogurt?"

Alex shook his head.

Alex's parents looked at each other and

shrugged their shoulders. Finally Dad spoke. "OK, Alex," he said. "What's up?"

"What?"

"Or perhaps I should say 'what's down?' " Dad continued. "since you're obviously down in the dumps. What's bothering you? Is it the horse?"

"Beanie's a hinny," Alex said gloomily. "Not a horse."

"OK," Dad continued, "Is it the hinny?"

Alex sighed deeply. Yes, he was upset about Beanie the hinny. And yet a small and confused part of him was excited this morning too. A horse of his very own! But was that good or bad when the horse was Beanie?

"You don't want Beanie." Mom said. "Is that the problem?"

"I don't know!" Alex said.

"Listen, Alex," Mom said. "This may surprise you, but I really didn't want a horse around here at first. After meeting Beanie, though, I think you should give him a chance."

"Maybe I don't like horses anymore," Alex said glumly.

"Beanie's a very lovable horse," Mom replied. "He's special. He's different from the rest."

"He's different, all right," Alex agreed.

Dad frowned. "Alex," he said. "I think you're paying too much attention to the way Beanie looks. He seems like a very nice animal. Remember, beauty is only skin deep."

"Skin is important," Alex argued.

"Remember how much you prayed for a horse of your own?" Mom said softly. "And now it looks like God is answering your prayer."

"I prayed for a *nice* horse," Alex said crossly, a part of him already feeling ashamed of his feelings. "I didn't pray for an ugly one."

"Alexander Jahns," Alex's father scolded. "You should know that appearance isn't important—not in people and not in animals, either. It's what's in the heart that counts."

"Are you telling me that you like Beanie too?" Alex asked.

Dad slowly nodded his head. "I think

you should give Beanie a chance," he said.

"Mom?" Alex asked.

"I think Beanie is an answer to prayer," Mom answered.

"I was praying for a different kind of horse," Alex sighed.

"Alex, God is much wiser than we are," Dad said, "and He'll choose what's best for you."

"I thought all things were possible for God," Alex said.

"They are," Dad agreed. "And sometimes the best possible thing is for us to let God have His way, even if at first we don't like the way things are going."

Alex rolled his eyes. He didn't understand his parents. For years they had been telling him he couldn't have a horse. Now they had met Beanie, and everything suddenly changed.

"I'm never going to love Beanie," Alex said.

"Maybe not," Dad replied. "But then again, maybe you will. God doesn't make mistakes, Alex." He heard the sound of a motor and looked out the window. "Here comes Grandpa's truck," he said. Then he hesitated. "But where's the horse trailer?"

Everyone hurried outside. Grandpa had planned to bring Beanie over in his horse trailer. But instead the hinny stood in the back of Grandpa's half-ton truck, peering calmly over the low box at the family below him.

"Where's the horse trailer?" Dad asked, staring at Beanie.

"I couldn't get it connected to the back of my truck," Grandpa replied. "Wrong size hitch, I guess."

"So you drove down the road like that?" Mom exclaimed.

"Uh-huh."

"Nobody hauls animals in the back of a truck," Dad said sternly. "It's dangerous."

"Dangerous?"

"The sides of the truck box only come to Beanie's knees," Dad continued. "He could have jumped out!"

"Or fallen out," Mom added.

"I didn't drive very fast," Grandpa said. "And I turned the corners very slowly."

"It was still dangerous," Dad insisted, "and I'm pretty sure it's against the law too."

Grandpa scratched his head sheepishly. "Against the law?" he asked.

"Yes," Dad replied. "I'm sure it's against the law to haul animals loose in the back of a truck."

"I drove only five miles," Grandpa said.

"Five miles or fifty miles," Mom said, "it's still dangerous. And we wouldn't want anything to happen to our little Beanie."

"Sorry," Grandpa said.

Beanie snorted loudly from his position above their heads.

"I don't think Beanie liked the trip very much, anyway," Grandpa said.

"Why not?" Alex asked.

"He had to keep his head down really low," Grandpa replied. "Otherwise he kept getting hit in the face by bugs."

"Bugs?"

"Haven't you ever seen the way your windshield looks in the summer, Alex?" Grandpa asked. "Bugs hit the glass, and—splat—they make a horrible mess! Poor Beanie had to keep his head down so that he didn't get hit by bugs."

Alex laughed in spite of himself.

Grandpa walked to the back of the truck and pulled down the end gate. "Okay, Beanie," he said, "we better let you out before we get in more trouble."

Beanie turned around carefully, making the truck sway back and forth. He walked to the edge of the open truck box, his hooves echoing on the heavy metal, and peered down at the ground below. Then with a surprisingly nimble jump, Beanie bounced out onto the grass.

"How did you ever get that poor animal loaded in the back of your truck, anyway?" Mom asked.

"It was easy," Grandpa said proudly.

"Easy?"

"Yep," Grandpa said. "I just opened the truck's end gate and told Beanie to jump in."

"And he did?" Dad asked. "Just like that?"

"Well, I did have to ask twice," Grandpa admitted.

"You're telling me that mule jumped into the back of the truck?" Dad said. "Just like that?"

"Hinnies are good jumpers," Grandpa said. "Why, mules and hinnies have their very own competition called 'The Coon Hunters' jump.' That's because they can jump straight up in the air from a standing start. Why, I once saw an old mule jump . . ."

Alex stroked Beanie's sleek back and smiled to himself. Beanie was a strange-looking animal, and in spite of Dad's lecture about looks not being that important, Alex still wasn't convinced Beanie was the horse for him.

But there was something interesting about an animal brave enough to ride in the back of a truck. If Beanie would do something like that for Grandpa, what would he do for Alex? What kind of adventures could the two have? Maybe . . .

The Black Stallion was smart and beautiful and fast, but there was no way *he* would have jumped into the back of a tiny half-ton truck and traveled five miles down the road ducking his head to avoid flying bugs!

Alex reached forward and grabbed Beanie's lead rope. The hinny raised his head and looked straight at Alex.

Then Beanie curled his lip and shook his head. It seemed to Alex that Beanie winked his long, brown eyelashes and smiled a big, horsy smile. It was all Alex could do to keep from laughing out loud when he saw a big, dead bug caught between Beanie's teeth!

CHAPTER

4

Alex Learns
to Ride

Alex spent all afternoon working with Beanie. At Foothills Camp he had learned the basics of caring for a horse, but now Alex had a real reason to concentrate. Grandpa showed Alex many new things. He learned how to position the saddle blanket smoothly so that there were no wrinkles, and how to set the saddle in place so Beanie's shoulders could move easily while he walked. Twice Alex tried to put on Beanie's bridle, but both times the leather ended up twisted and lumpy, so Grandpa finished the job— much to both Alex's and Beanie's relief!

After saddling Beanie, Alex practiced mounting and dismounting smoothly. That was something that Alex found easy to do on Beanie. With the hinny's short legs, and Alex's long ones, getting on and off wasn't a problem.

Next Alex worked on riding the hinny around the yard. Grandpa showed Alex how Beanie had been trained to neck rein. "You hold both reins in one hand," Grandpa said. "And you don't have to pull on the inside rein. Just lay the rein on his neck, and Beanie will turn away from the pressure."

Alex tried Grandpa's suggestion and was pleased to see that it worked. Before long, Alex was walking and trotting Beanie up and down the gravel lane.

That was fun! For a moment Alex even closed his eyes and let the fresh air rush across his face. Beanie's gait was surprisingly smooth, and Alex hardly bounced, even at a brisk trot. For a moment Alex could even imagine he was riding the perfect horse—tall and black and sleek and smooth—except when Alex opened his eyes, it was all a dream.

It's like my dream the other night, Alex thought with a frown. *My beautiful horse has turned into a hamster. Or a hinny!*

Before putting Beanie away in the corral, Alex carefully cleaned all the rocks and pebbles out of his hooves. He brushed the dried sweat off Beanie's back and ran a comb through Beanie's thin mane and tail.

"He looks perfect," Grandpa said when Alex showed him the now-sparkling clean hinny.

Perfect, all right, Alex thought, rolling his eyes. *Perfectly ugly!*

"You did a really good job caring for your horse today," Grandpa said as he watched Alex lead Beanie over to the wooden corral that was to be Beanie's new home. "You were a very responsible horse owner."

"Beanie isn't a horse," Alex said. "He's a hinny." But Alex had to admit that he had learned a lot in one day. In fact, he had done more with Beanie in a day than he had done with the camp horses in an entire week.

I know that I'll never love Beanie, Alex thought. *But I can learn a lot from him. And I can have fun with him until I get a real horse of my own.*

Alex held Beanie while Grandpa swung the wooden corral gate open. Then he lead the hinny inside and slipped the halter off Beanie's head.

Beanie nuzzled Alex's hands and then walked to the center of the corral and pawed the ground with his hoof. Little puffs of dust rose. With a satisfied grunt, Beanie flopped over onto his side and began to roll.

Alex laughed as he watched the hinny roll from side to side. Beanie grunted loudly, rubbing his head and shoulders firmly in the soft dirt. When he finally got to his feet, Beanie shook firmly, sending bits of dirt and grass flying across the corral.

"Beanie grunts like a pig!" Alex laughed.

Grandpa nodded.

"Does Beanie neigh like a horse?" Alex asked while Grandpa fastened the gate shut. "Or does he hee-haw like a donkey?"

"I don't know," Grandpa said. "Beanie's always quiet."

"Always quiet?"

"Yep," Grandpa said. "Other than an occasional grunt or snort, he never makes a sound."

Alex's rubbed his tired legs. "Thanks, Grandpa," he said. "I learned a lot today."

"It was fun for me, too," Grandpa said. "I just knew you'd learn to love Beanie. He's perfect for you."

Alex shrugged and didn't reply. After all, what was there to say?

That evening, Alex said his prayers and then swung his tired legs into bed. Through the bedroom window he could dimly see Beanie ambling around the corral. It gave Alex a strange, mixed-up feeling to see a horse outside his window! There was a swift rush of pleasure—a horse of his own! But then a gloomy, heavy feeling of disappointment followed.

The "horse" was only Beanie—ugly and small—and not exactly a horse at all. Beanie was a hinny.

But maybe it wouldn't matter. Alex would keep Beanie just long enough to become a good horse rider. Then he would be able to handle a better horse—this time the picture-perfect steed that Alex had prayed for.

Beanie wasn't all bad. He was very well trained, and yet he still had a mind of his own. He was smart and clever and trusting at the same time. Beanie was special. He was a horse that thought he was a person. In fact, if Beanie *had* been a person, he probably would have been the type of person that Alex would have liked for a friend. He would be smart. Funny. Interesting.

But Beanie wasn't a person. Beanie was nothing more than a funny-looking hinny. And nothing could change that.

Not even Alex's prayers.

CHAPTER
5

Beanie Escapes!

The next morning, the wooden corral gate was open, and Beanie was gone!

Alex looked in surprise at the empty corral and then quickly around the farmyard. He remembered his grandpa's nimble fingers as they looped the chain around the hook. The gate had been closed. So how had Beanie escaped?

"Beanie!" Alex called. His heart pounded so hard he felt dizzy for a moment. What a terrible horse owner he was! Losing his horse the very first day!

Where would Beanie go?

Alex immediately knew the answer to that question.

Beanie would go back to his old farm.

With a last frantic look around the yard, Alex raced back to the house, calling loudly for his parents.

Dad came out of the bathroom, his face half shaved and his hair still standing on end. "What's all the noise about?" he wanted to know.

When Alex explained the situation, Dad didn't hesitate. He set down his razor on the kitchen table and quickly gathered his car keys.

"Don't worry, Alex," Dad reassured him. "We'll find Beanie."

"Are you coming, Mom?" Alex asked.

Mom shook her head. "I'll be no help finding a missing horse," she said. "But I'll pray for you. So don't worry, everything will be okay."

But Alex couldn't stop worrying.

It was a five-mile trip from their house to the Jacobson farm. Beanie would have to travel down a busy, oiled road and then cross an even busier highway. There would be dozens of vehicles that could hit him.

Beanie could get lost. He could get tangled in a heap of barbed wire. He could fall down a ravine and break a leg.

Okay, Alex thought quickly. *There aren't any ravines around here, so I probably don't have to worry about that. But almost anything else could happen!*

Alex and his father carefully scanned the countryside as they drove down the road. Alex kept his window rolled down, and every so often he would lean outside and call Beanie's name.

There was no answer.

Beanie won't answer, Alex thought glumly as they came to the first corner and turned west. *Beanie's always quiet. I couldn't hear him anyway, unless he grunts loud enough for me to hear from the car! Plus, Beanie doesn't know me very well. He probably wouldn't come when I call, anyway.*

Soon they came to the busy highway. Dad had to wait for a few moments until the traffic thinned enough that he could turn to the left. Now Alex became even more anxious. Car after car whizzed past their vehicle.

Beanie could be anywhere. He could be standing in the middle of the road while vehicles drove straight toward him. He could be lying somewhere, unconscious in the ditch.

Dad's knuckles were white as he gripped the steering wheel. "Why didn't you shut the gate?" he asked.

"Grandpa did shut the gate!" Alex said. "Honest."

Before long they pulled into the Jacobson's yard. Alex hopped out of the car and raced toward Beanie's old pasture.

But the pasture was empty.

Beanie wasn't grazing in the deep grass. He wasn't hiding behind the willow bushes or near the deserted water trough.

Beanie wasn't there.

And they hadn't seen him anywhere along the roadside.

So where could Beanie be?

"I'm going to phone Grandpa Stevens," Dad finally said. "We should have done that at the beginning. Maybe Grandpa will know where to look next."

But his cell phone wouldn't work. Dad let out a long sigh. "OK," he said, "we'll have to use the phone at home."

They were almost home when Alex suddenly glimpsed something brown and white at the back of their neighbor's pasture. "Dad!" Alex shouted, "stop the car!"

Dad slammed on the brakes.

"There!" Alex shouted, pointing. "I see Beanie!"

But when they got closer to the pasture, they saw that the brown-and-white animal was nothing more than a cow!

Alex was surprised at how close to tears he suddenly felt—surprised because nine-year-old boys don't cry very often. And surprised because he really couldn't understand why he was so upset. Of course he didn't want Beanie to be hurt. Alex didn't want any animal hurt. But Beanie really wasn't that special.

Was he?

Another surprise happened when Dad parked the car in front of the house. Mom stood outside the house with Beanie beside her, his eyes half closed as she scratched his shoulder!

"Beanie!" Alex exclaimed, scrambling out of the car. "Where did you find him?"

"I didn't find him," Mom replied. "He found me."

"What?"

"I was clearing dishes off the kitchen table, and I heard a strange sound," Mom explained. "It was Beanie, staring in the living-room window. He had his face right up against the glass, trying to see if anyone was inside."

"Why would he do that?"

"I think he was looking for you," Mom told Alex.

"More likely looking for *you*!" Alex snorted.

"Why didn't you just catch him?" Dad asked.

"You've got to be kidding!" Mom answered. "I don't like horses, and even if I did, I certainly don't know how to put his halter on."

"But Mom, Beanie could have run away again," Alex said.

"Run away? I don't think Beanie's planning to run away. When I walk a step, he follows me. When I stop, Beanie stops. It's almost like he's my shadow." Mom nodded her head to make a point, and as if on cue Beanie nodded his head, too.

"So why didn't you just walk into the corral with Beanie and shut the gate?" Dad asked. "Surely you can shut a gate even if you don't like horses."

"All right, Mr. Horse Expert," Mom replied. "I'll have you know that I *did* lock Beanie in the corral."

"Then why is he still standing here with you?"

"Because he opened the gate and let himself out," Mom said.

"Really?" Alex asked.

"Really," Mom told him. "I'll show you."

Alex slipped the halter over Beanie's long ears and lead the hinny back to the corral. Mom shut the gate and pointed to the chain.

"He took the chain in his teeth," she said, "then he pulled upward—and the chain came right off the hook."

"You probably didn't put the chain on right," Dad told her.

"I did so," Mom insisted. "I tell you, Beanie can open the gate."

Everyone stepped back to see if Beanie would do it again.

Beanie ignored them. Instead he walked over to the center of the corral and prepared to roll.

"Fine," Mom shouted at him, "Make me a liar, Beanie!"

"I think you were dreaming," Dad grinned.

"I wasn't dreaming. He opened the gate as easily as you could. Just one little pull, and it came right off the hook."

"Well, then we'll have to outsmart our escape artist, won't we?" Dad said. He disappeared for a few minutes and returned with a long piece of heavy twine. "We'll just make sure that our little gate opener doesn't escape again." He carefully tied the gate shut.

Later in the afternoon, Grandpa came out to the farm. He had Alex and Beanie practice their paces. They saddled, and Alex tried again to bridle Beanie without success.

It wasn't Beanie's fault, Alex had to admit. The hinny opened his mouth wide whenever the shiny silver bit came his direction. It was almost like he was trying to help Alex.

But somehow Alex couldn't get things coordinated. Either the chin strap would get tangled and end up in Beanie's mouth, or the leather side pieces would twist around so that the bit wouldn't reach.

But even if bridling didn't go so well, Alex did learn some more things. He learned how to make Beanie back and how to bend his neck properly so he could turn sharply, and he even managed to get the hinny to canter for a short distance down the lane.

Cantering was a lot of fun. Beanie was like a well-used rocking chair. He might be lumpy and funny-looking, but he was smooth and comfortable. Probably even more comfortable than the Black Stallion.

Alex was grinning while he put the little hinny away. And he was still smiling as he closed the gate carefully, making certain the chain was over the hook and that the rope was tied properly. Then he forked a section of sweet-smelling hay over the fence and watched as Beanie began to eat.

Having a horse of his own was more fun than Alex had imagined. And as he studied Beanie carefully, he thought the little animal was beginning to look a bit more handsome. Somehow Beanie's ears didn't seem so long and silly anymore. And his big head was also beginning to look better. It didn't look so much like a bucket as it had at first. It looked more like a horse's head—a big horse's head, maybe, but certainly not like a bucket.

And there was something about Beanie's color that was downright pretty. The soft, white fur with the big blotches of brown was different. It was special.

After all, a lot of horses were plain brown or gray or black.

But there was nothing plain about Beanie. Nothing plain at all.

CHAPTER

6

Free Again!

The corral was empty again the next morning. The chain was off the hook, and the long piece of rope was nowhere in sight. Neither was Beanie.

Alex was frightened, but this time he wasn't as frightened as he had been the day before.

Any horse that is smart enough to undo knots and open gates is smart enough to watch out for traffic, Alex thought. *Maybe.*

Alex jogged into the house and called his parents. They searched all around the yard and the nearby pastures, but Beanie was nowhere to be found.

"Should we drive over to the Jacobson farm?" Alex finally asked.

Dad shrugged his shoulders. "I don't know," he admitted.

"Let's wait a bit longer," Mom suggested. "Beanie knows where we live, and I think he'll come looking for us."

"But the road . . ." Alex couldn't finish the sentence.

"Enough!" Dad said firmly. "We'll find him lazing around somewhere, and we'll bring him home. And this time I'm going to make sure he doesn't escape again."

"What are you going to do?" Mom asked. "Handcuff the poor thing?"

"Maybe I will," Dad replied. "Maybe I will."

The family ate breakfast quickly. Mom got up twice and went to the front room window, hoping to find Beanie staring in at her. But Beanie didn't appear.

"OK, Alex," Dad said when breakfast was over. "Let's drive to the Jacobson's. I suspect Beanie would have come looking for your mother already if he were anywhere nearby."

Alex was just climbing into the car when something caught his eye. There—down by the garden—was something brown and white. Could it be Beanie?

"It's probably just a cow," Dad said.

"We don't have any cows, Dad," Alex replied. "Remember?"

It was Beanie. He was almost out of sight, lying in the grass underneath the big crab apple tree. A pile of apples was stacked in front of the hinny, and as they watched, Beanie reached his muzzle forward and rolled another fallen apple into the pile.

"He thinks he's a squirrel, storing food for the winter," Dad said with a disgusted sigh.

Beanie blinked his big brown eyes innocently.

"And there's the rope," Dad said.

The long piece of twine used to close the gate lay nearby. "How did that get here?" Alex wondered.

"Beanie probably planned to hide it under his pile of apples," Alex's father said. He picked up the rope and made it into a rough halter. Then he slipped the halter onto Beanie's head and passed the end of the rope to Alex.

"There you go," Dad said. "Now let's take this beast back to the corral."

Alex looked at Beanie lying peacefully beside him. *What would happen if I sat on Beanie's back?* Alex thought.

Without hesitating, Alex slipped one leg over the hinny's back and sat down.

"What are you doing?" Dad wanted to know.

"Beanie feels just like a big sofa," Alex said.

"A horse-hair sofa," Dad laughed.

Then Beanie decided to stand up. Alex felt himself being carried upward as the horse struggled to his feet. Once Beanie was standing, he gave himself a firm shake—almost bouncing Alex off his back—before slowly ambling back to the corral.

Alex's mother scratched the hinny's ears. "Don't worry, Beanie," she said, "you can stay in the corral, and I'll bring the apples to you. OK?"

"Don't worry," Dad said. "He won't be getting out again!"

Grandpa appeared a few hours later. He set up an obstacle course for Beanie and Alex. Alex practiced guiding Beanie over a ramp and then zigzagged him back and forth between some barrels. They even jumped a small jump that Grandpa made out of some logs.

"He jumps really well," Alex exclaimed.

"Any horse that can leap into the back of a truck can certainly jump that tiny log," Grandpa agreed.

Jumping was almost like flying, and Alex found himself having more fun than ever. For an awkward-looking animal, Beanie was actually very coordinated. He slipped between the barrels easily and over the little jumps as though he had done it all his life.

Dad helped Alex shut the corral gate behind Beanie that evening. "Beanie won't be getting out tonight," Dad declared, showing Alex the snap he had attached to the chain. "Beanie may have sharp teeth, but there's one thing he doesn't have."

"What?" Alex asked.

"Thumbs," Dad explained. "And unless he has a thumb, he won't be opening this gate anymore."

Alex tried it himself. His father was right. Unless Alex used his thumb and fingers together, he couldn't open the snap.

The corral gate was still closed the next morning.

But Beanie was gone again!

When Alex looked carefully, he found a second, smaller gate on the far side of the corral. It was standing wide open. Beanie had slipped his head through the gate, and by lifting upward, he had managed to swing the wire loop off the post!

This time Alex walked straight to the garden to look for Beanie.

Beanie was by the carrot patch, pawing at the ground. A pile of carrot tops lay around his feet.

Alex slipped the halter on Beanie and picked up a half-eaten carrot. "Come on, boy," Alex said, holding the carrot in front of the hinny. Beanie followed peacefully.

Dad grumbled as he put a chain around the second gate. "That had better do it," he said. "This chain is expensive."

Later Alex saw his mother feeding Beanie another carrot through the corral rails. "Poor boy," she cooed. "You were just hungry, weren't you?"

Beanie seemed to enjoy living at the Jahns' household, especially with all that tasty food within easy reach. But how would he get out tomorrow?

CHAPTER

7

Beanie the Barrel Racer

Beanie was in the corral the next morning. Alex thought the hinny looked a bit disappointed in himself, so he tossed him an extra flake of hay. "That should cheer you up," Alex said.

Beanie sighed and ate the hay slowly. It was clear that he didn't think hay was as tasty as apples and carrots.

Beanie didn't escape from his corral again that summer. Instead he stayed home and worked with Alex and Grandpa Stevens every day.

With a lot of practice, Alex managed to learn to bridle Beanie by himself. He also learned to canter the hinny, and to stop and turn him easily. When that started to become routine, Grandpa set up a barrel-racing course and explained the pattern.

"It really isn't very difficult," he told Alex. "There are three barrels, right? You start at the left barrel and circle it. Then you go to the next barrel and circle it the opposite direction. Then you race down to the farthest barrel there, turn the corner, and come back here across the finish line."

"Do we go fast?" Alex asked.

Grandpa shook his head. "Not at first," he said. "You need to practice the pattern slowly. You don't want Beanie to rush. You want him to think. He needs to turn the corners sharply without hitting the barrels. When he gets better, then you start going faster. Sometimes."

Barrel racing was even more fun than jumping.

Within a few weeks, Beanie and Alex had the pattern down perfectly. Beanie would gallop to the first barrel, and when

Alex cued him, Beanie would spin around the barrel and race across to the second one. Beanie's short little legs would dig into the ground as he whirled around that barrel and charged down to the third. At the last barrel there would be a final quick turn and then a dash down to the finish line.

Beanie seemed to enjoy the race as much as Alex did. Of course, Alex was careful to do a lot of other things with the hinny so he wouldn't become too bored. But Alex enjoyed barrel racing so much, it was hard for him to stop practicing.

One evening Alex's parents came down to the ring to watch the pair work. Alex trotted the pattern twice, and then on the last trip through he put Beanie into a hard run. When the hinny finally came to a halt, spraying dirt everywhere, all three adults clapped loudly.

"I can't believe it!" Dad exclaimed. "I wouldn't have believed Beanie was so fast if I hadn't seen it myself."

"Beanie deserves a treat," Mom said. "Don't you, Beanie Boy?" She fumbled in her coat pocket. Beanie had been standing quietly beside Grandpa, but when Mrs. Jahns spoke his name, he walked forward, nodding his head. *Yes, I do deserve a treat, don't I?* Beanie seemed to be saying.

Mom fed several pieces of apple to Beanie. When he was finished, Beanie put his head against her happily.

"Careful," Mom said. "I don't like horses. Remember?"

"Barrel racing is a good sport," Grandpa said. "It isn't the biggest—or even the fastest—horse that wins. The horse that wins is the horse that turns and runs the pattern best. And Beanie has an excellent turn. He's always right where he's supposed to be."

"Do you think Beanie could win a real barrel race?" Alex asked, sliding down from Beanie's back.

"Of course Beanie could win a real barrel race," Grandpa declared.

"Against all the big horses?" Alex wanted to know.

"Didn't I just say that it isn't the biggest horse that wins barrel races?" Grandpa asked.

"Yeah, but . . ."

"And didn't I tell you that Roger Jacobson rode Beanie at gymkhana races?" Grandpa asked. "They always did very well at barrel racing."

"You mean Beanie has barrel raced before this?" Alex asked.

"Of course he has," Grandpa laughed. "And he can pole bend and keyhole and do a lot of other races, too."

"Then why did you make us practice so much?"

"Because *you* didn't know what to do," Grandpa replied. "And Beanie hadn't barrel raced for a few years, either. But now the two of you are performing very well."

Beanie was asleep now, his big head resting comfortably against Mrs. Jahns. She was stroking his long ears softly, exactly the way Beanie liked best.

"Mom, you should take Beanie for a ride," Alex suddenly offered.

She stepped backward so quickly

Beanie opened his eyes. "I don't ride horses," Mom exclaimed.

"But you could ride a hinny," Alex said.

Mom laughed and shook her head. "I don't ride hinnies, either," she said.

"Beanie would take good care of you," Alex assured her.

His mother hesitated and then shook her head. "That's the problem with you men," she said. "Remember, I said you'd have to be crazy to like horses. And I'm never going to be that crazy."

That night Alex lay in bed, thinking.

Alex would like to barrel race. In a few weeks there would be a gymkhana at the local riding club. Alex had gone every year to watch the races. One of his classmates, Tyler Klaus, rode a big sorrel quarter horse named Ginger, and most years they had collected a handful of colorful ribbons.

Alex would like to win a ribbon himself.

This year he had a horse of his own. And he had a horse that could do the races.

But there was one little problem.

Everyone would stop and stare at Beanie. Alex had almost forgotten how unusual Beanie looked. Alex didn't even notice the long dachshund body and the short, little legs anymore. The floppy ears, the lumpy head, the scraggly mane and tail—they didn't seem to matter much now.

Beanie was smart. Beanie was fun. Beanie was Alex's horse—at least for the summer.

But it would matter to Tyler Klaus and the other kids. They'd stop and stare at Beanie. They'd laugh and make fun of Alex.

But Alex couldn't stop thinking about the ribbons.

Why, maybe they could win several ribbons! Alex would need to learn how to pole bend, but Grandpa could teach him that. They could set up a pole bending course at the back of the field, and maybe there'd still be room to set up a keyhole pattern. They would need some chalk or something to mark the pattern on the ground and then . . .

Suddenly Alex thought of something else. Winners of the gymkhana races received prize money as well as ribbons! Alex could win a lot of money. He could put the money toward a new saddle blanket to replace the old worn-out one they were using. Or he could buy a real pair of cowboy boots instead of the faded hiking boots he was still wearing.

Or Alex could put the money towards a new horse!

Do I really want another horse? Alex asked himself. He didn't know the answer. Besides, it would take a lot of money to buy another horse.

Alex flopped over on the bed and closed his eyes. He pictured himself turning the first barrel, the second, the third. He and Beanie were sprinting toward the finish line.

They won!

Alex and Beanie picked up another first place ribbon!

Once again, Alex and Beanie had outraced everyone—even Tyler and Ginger.

But it was only a dream, and Alex knew it took more than dreams to succeed.

God, You could help me, Alex prayed. *I know Beanie will never be a pretty horse. I haven't even prayed that you would make him look better. But would it be okay if I prayed that You make Beanie fast? I really would like to win a race.*

Was that a good prayer? Alex wasn't so sure. But if he didn't ask, then how could God answer?

CHAPTER

8

Chase the Dragon and Other Races

Alex thought constantly about the upcoming gymkhana races. Grandpa Stevens helped him set up the pole bending course and used paint to mark the keyhole pattern on the hard-packed ground.

Alex rode Beanie as often as possible. Most days they worked the patterns slowly, concentrating on smooth turns. Some days they galloped the pattern once or twice and then returned to working slowly. Other days they avoided the ring and, instead, went for long trail rides across the nearby fields.

Alex was proud of Beanie. They had both learned a lot this summer. Beanie could now side pass and pivot on his back legs. He could move effortlessly from a walk into a lope and then slow down just as quickly back to a walk again. He could jump small obstacles easily.

Sometimes it seemed that Beanie could do anything he wanted to do.

But Alex was still having a hard time deciding whether or not he should enter the gymkhana races.

It would be fun. It would be a chance to win ribbons and money. But it was also a chance for Alex to be laughed at. The thought of Tyler Klaus pointing at Beanie's long ears and potbelly was more than Alex could stand.

What should he do? For a long time there didn't seem to be an answer to Alex's question.

It was Alex's mother who helped him decide.

Mom had been shopping in Stettler, and when she entered the house with an armload of bags, she began to call Alex's name excitedly. Alex put down his book and trudged into the kitchen.

"What do you need?" Alex asked, expecting a chore.

"You'll never guess what I have for you!" Mom announced. She beamed as she passed Alex a large, brown box.

Alex couldn't imagine what was inside. It wasn't his birthday, and he knew the family didn't have a lot of extra money to spare.

Inside the box was a pair of beautiful, black cowboy boots. Alex held them up with an excited shout. They were shiny black and glistened in the light. He slipped his feet inside the boots. They were a perfect fit!

"Thank you!" Alex finally managed to say.

Mom grinned back at him. "These boots are an answer to prayer," she said.

"An answer to prayer?"

"I wanted you to have proper boots for the gymkhana races," she told him. "But I just didn't know where I'd get the money. Then I saw the western wear store in

Stettler is going out of business. There was one pair of boots left! These! As soon as I saw them, I knew they'd be perfect for you. And they cost only twenty dollars!"

Alex knew then that he'd have to enter the races.

Maybe twenty dollars wasn't a lot of money for a pair of real leather boots, but it was a lot of money for his family to spare. Alex would have to enter the races and wear the boots. Even if Tyler Klaus did laugh at him.

Strangely enough, Alex felt a rush of relief once he had decided to go to the races. Not knowing what to do had been the hardest thing, he decided as he gazed at the new boots. He would go to the races, and he would do his best.

Hopefully no one would laugh at Beanie. If they did, he'd just do his best to ignore them.

Alex filled out the entry form the next day with Grandpa's help. Alex entered almost every race in the ten-and-under age group. There was, of course, the barrel race and pole bending and keyhole. Then there were several other races that Alex had never heard of—one called musical poles and one called chase the dragon.

Grandpa shrugged his shoulders when he read the name of the last race. "I have no idea either," he told Alex, "but it can't hurt to try, can it?"

Alex was up early the day of the race. Grandpa arrived before seven o'clock to help load Beanie in the stock trailer. Before long they were at the crowded fairgrounds.

Alex was so nervous he could hardly talk as he brushed Beanie. He kept tripping over his new cowboy boots, and a few minutes earlier he had spilled juice down the front of his shiny blue western shirt.

Beanie, on the other hand, didn't seem the least bit nervous. He pulled wisps of hay out of the bag tied in front of him and ignored all the excitement.

Grandpa had parked the truck and trailer at the far edge of the fairgrounds, so no one seemed to notice the funny-looking hinny at first. It wasn't until Alex rode Beanie around the field to warm him up that everyone looked his way.

Even the announcer commented on Beanie. When it was time for the first race—which was pole bending—the announcer commented, "There's that donkey that Roger Jacobson entered in some races a few years ago!"

"That's not a donkey," Grandpa corrected the announcer loudly. "That's a hinny. And you'd better get a good look at him now because once he gets moving you'll hardly be able to see him!"

Alex's nervousness made for a less-than-perfect pole bending run. Alex hesitated and turned the little hinny too slowly, so they crossed the finish line with a time that didn't bring home any ribbons.

Tyler Klaus, carrying his bright, blue ribbon, waved at Alex as he trotted past.

"Never mind, Beanie," Alex said, rubbing the animal's sleek shoulder. "That was my fault, wasn't it? We'll do better in the next race."

The keyhole race did go better. This time Alex was not so nervous as he galloped Beanie down the arena to the narrow path in front of him. He concentrated on what lay ahead. *Enter the path, stop quickly, turn around without stepping out of the pattern, and then gallop back out the same way you came in,* he repeated to himself.

Keyhole wasn't Beanie's best race, probably because he and Alex had been practicing it only for a few weeks, but Alex was thrilled when they won a fourth place ribbon!

There was a short break while the other age groups ran through the keyhole pattern, and then some adults stepped into the ring to set up the barrel racing pattern.

Alex and Beanie were the last pair to compete in the barrel racing, so Alex stood at the back of the group and watched as one horse after another raced around the pattern. Some pairs had obviously not practiced very much. Those horses ran wide around the barrels or knocked them down. One horse reared and didn't finish the race.

Tyler and Ginger had an excellent round, with a time of seventeen and a half seconds. Tyler grinned at Alex as they trotted past. Tyler still looked neat and tidy, and Ginger's long mane swayed in the faint breeze. For a moment Alex felt a tug at his heart. He loved horses— everything about them—the way they looked, the way they moved, even the way they smelled. And Ginger was exactly the sort of horse Alex had wanted.

Alex looked away. *Remember,* he told himself, *it isn't the biggest or fastest horse that wins. It's the horse that turns the pattern the best.*

He sent up a quick prayer: *God, please help us win the race.* Then he thought for a moment. Maybe that wasn't a fair prayer.

Dear God, please help Beanie and me to do our best. And help me be a good sport. Amen. Somehow that felt better.

Alex was almost relaxed when it was his turn to enter the arena.

Everything happened in a whirl! He and Beanie crossed the starting line at a hard gallop, turned a perfect first barrel, and then raced to the second barrel. They turned that one smoothly, too.

They were almost at the third barrel when it happened.

There was a loud *ka-boom,* and the announcer's microphone began to screech wildly!

Alex lost his concentration for a moment. *What was that noise?* He hesitated at the third barrel. *Now? Should we turn now?*

But Beanie didn't hesitate.

The hinny spun around the last barrel, without waiting for Alex's cue, and streaked towards the finish line.

When the dust cleared, the announcer's voice boomed loudly, "Seventeen seconds even!"

It wasn't until Alex and Beanie had collected their first-place ribbon that Alex learned what had happened. The announcer's folding, wooden table had collapsed against the arena wall, taking two chairs and the microphone with it!

"I don't think any other horse would have run so well with all that racket!" Grandpa told Alex.

Mom fed Beanie an apple. "He's the best horse in the world," she said proudly.

This time Alex didn't correct his mother. Because Beanie *was* a really good horse, even if he was just a funny-looking hinny.

Musical poles ended up being a lot of fun. The audience laughed and cheered as pairs of horses and riders trotted around a big circle of poles in time to the music. When the music stopped, the rider raced to the nearest pole, jumped off, and grabbed the pole. If he missed a pole, he was disqualified. If the horse ran away, its rider was disqualified, too.

Slowly the pairs thinned out, as one person after another missed a pole. So far, Alex was managing well. Beanie's short legs made it easy for Alex to jump off, and Beanie's calm attitude was a big help in the crowded ring.

Finally it came down to one pole and two riders—Tyler and Ginger and Alex and Beanie. As they circled the ring, Alex concentrated on the music, waiting for it to quit so he could gallop to the last pole.

"Go, Beanie Boy!" Mom called as the pair trotted past her.

Suddenly, Beanie saw Mrs. Jahns. He thought about her pockets filled with apples and the wonderful way she scratched his forehead.

Beanie slammed on the brakes and reached over toward her for a pleasant scratch. That might not have been a big problem, except at that very moment the music quit!

By the time Alex had gathered the reins and pushed Beanie forward, it was too late. Tyler stood by the last pole with Ginger at his side.

Everyone laughed as Alex collected his second-place ribbon. "You're a good boy," Alex told Beanie, "but a bit too greedy!" Alex wasn't disappointed. A second-place ribbon in that race seemed very good indeed.

Everyone enjoyed chase the dragon more than all the other races put together. It was a hilarious race in which one of the rider's parents was the dragon and had to run across the ring and jump a series of low jumps while the rider galloped after him on his horse. If a rider passed his parent, he was disqualified. If a rider bumped his parent, he was disqualified. Otherwise, the rules were simple—the fastest time won.

"Mom, you just have to be my dragon," Alex begged.

Mom shook her head firmly. "Get your father," she said. "I'm too old to race around the ring with a crazy hinny running behind me!"

"But Mom," Alex argued, "Beanie loves you. He'll run as fast as he can to keep up with you."

Grandpa and Dad agreed with Alex. So after much begging, Mom finally agreed to be the dragon.

They were a perfect team. Alex hadn't realized how fast his mother could run until he galloped Beanie after her across the ring. They had just crossed the last little jump and the finish line when Mrs. Jahns collapsed in front of them. Although she was laughing so hard tears streamed down her face, she had twisted her ankle, and it obviously hurt. In fact, Alex noticed his mother was barely putting any weight on it as she limped to the front to stand by Alex and Beanie when they collected their ribbon and prize money.

CHAPTER

9

Beanie
Goes Home

Alex carefully brushed Beanie's sweaty back and then left the hinny tied to the stock trailer while the family went to the ring to enjoy refreshments.

"Free pop and potato chips for all the contestants," the announcer boomed, "and that includes all our dragons too."

Mom rubbed her ankle. "I'm going home," she said. "My ankle really hurts. I'd like to put some ice on it."

They agreed that Mom would take the car home and the others would follow later with the truck and trailer. Alex waved goodbye to his mother and then hurried over to the cooler to collect a cold orange soda.

Tyler Klaus was there already, looking hot and sweaty even with a cold pop in his hand. "How many ribbons did you end up with, Alex?" Tyler asked.

"Four," Alex answered. "Two firsts, a second, and fourth."

"Not bad—for a beginner," Tyler said. He had won two firsts and three seconds. "But even if you had beat me, it wouldn't matter," Tyler continued. "I'd rather ride Ginger—and lose—than ride an ugly horse like yours and win."

Alex tried to pretend that the comment hadn't hurt, but it had. He wandered away from Tyler, helped himself to a bag of potato chips, and visited with a few other kids before deciding it was time to go.

But when Alex got back to the stock trailer, his grandpa and father were standing there looking bewildered— Beanie was nowhere to be seen!

Hinny, halter, and rope—everything was missing!

Alex looked around the fairgrounds frantically. Where would Beanie go? He could be anywhere, tucked behind a truck or trailer or something. Maybe he was eating another horse's hay or grain.

Or maybe he was already on the road, heading home.

"He was here just an hour ago," Alex said. "How far could he travel?"

"Are you sure you tied him up?" Dad asked when he returned breathlessly from a quick trip around the fair grounds.

"I did," Alex insisted. "With the quick release knot that Grandpa taught me."

"Quick release knot," Grandpa said thoughtfully. "I suppose it *was* quick release, all right. I should have known that a smart animal like Beanie could untie that knot."

"Well, he's not here," Dad said. "Alex, load your saddle and other stuff into the truck quickly. We'll have to go looking for your missing horse."

In a few minutes they were ready to go. Grandpa left a message with the announcer to phone them if Beanie returned to the fairgrounds, and then they drove away with a roar.

Would Beanie follow the road home? It was only about four miles to home, but it was a road that Beanie had never traveled before.

Would Beanie go as far as the first farmhouse and then stop to check out the garden? Would he be asleep underneath someone's apple tree? Was he trotting down the center of the road in the path of traffic?

Or even worse, maybe Beanie hadn't run away. Maybe someone had stolen him!

Before today, Alex hadn't thought that anyone else would have ever wanted Beanie. Now Alex realized that Beanie was the type of horse that a lot of people would want. He was fast. He was smart. He was lovable.

But he was missing.

Alex didn't want another horse. He didn't want the Black Stallion or Flicka or Misty anymore.

He wanted his own little hinny, big, bucket head and all.

"If you were a hinny, where would you go?" Dad asked as he steered the truck and trailer out of the sports grounds.

"Beanie would go home," Grandpa said firmly.

"To the Jacobson's?" Alex asked.

"No, silly," Grandpa said. "Home. To your place."

"To the garden," Dad said.

"To Mom," Alex said.

Both men nodded their heads.

"But would Beanie be able to find his way home?" Alex asked.

"I think so," Grandpa said. "But I don't know if he'd follow the road or if he'd take the shortcut across country. If he goes across country, he could save almost a mile. But then again, he could get lost or blocked by a fence."

They drove slowly down the gravel roads. Alex leaned his head out the truck window and called loudly for the hinny. But Beanie was nowhere in sight.

Alex began to think. God had given

him Beanie, even when Alex really hadn't wanted the little animal. God *had* known what was best, even when Alex thought God was wrong.

Alex should have trusted God then. And he should trust God now. God could take care of Beanie.

Alex loved Beanie, but he could leave him in God's care. Alex took a deep breath and felt his pounding heart begin to slow a little.

With God all things are possible, Alex thought.

"Let's hope he got home before we did," Dad said as they finally turned down the long driveway to their farm.

Suddenly everyone pointed ahead. "Look!"

Beanie was ambling down the lane. *And Mom was riding him!*

"Your mother's riding a horse!" Dad said to Alex in awe.

"Beanie's not a horse, Dad." Alex reminded him, "He's a hinny."

They pulled up slowly beside Mrs. Jahns. She turned and grinned at them.

"Well," she said, "it's about time you men got home. I thought I was going to have to do all the work around here—as usual!"

"Where did you find him?"

"How did you get on?"

"Doesn't your ankle hurt, Mom?"

Mrs. Jahns laughed. "I had just put ice on my ankle when I saw something moving near the garden. I knew it was Beanie. By the time I got there, he had laid down and was getting ready to have a little nap."

"I imagine he's tired," Alex said.

"He's raced all day and then traveled four miles," Dad said, "so he should be a little tired."

"My ankle was really hurting by the time I caught Beanie," Mom said. "And suddenly I decided, *Why walk when Beanie can carry me?* So I climbed onto his back, he stood up, and here we are."

"Mom," Alex said, "I can't believe it! You're finally riding a horse."

"I don't see what the big deal is," Mom answered. "You'd have to be crazy not to like Beanie. He'll take good care of me."

With a flick of her wrist, Mom steered the hinny away from the truck and across the lawn to the corral. Alex shook his head as he watched them go. "Wow," he whispered, "with God all things *are* possible, aren't they!"

Alex was amazed to think that his horse-hating mother had become Beanie's best friend. But something even more amazing had happened this summer.

God had given Alex a present that he hadn't wanted at first. But now Alex had to admit that God had been right. Beanie was the perfect horse—the perfect hinny—for Alex. God had seen past the long ears and the bucket head. He had seen Beanie's heart.

Alex hurried across the lawn and helped his mother dismount. Then he gave Beanie's neck a enormous hug.

Thank you God, Alex prayed silently, *for a horse of my own!*

If you enjoyed this book, you'll enjoy these other books in the **Julius and Friends** series:

Julius, the Perfectly Pesky Pet Parrot
VeraLee Wiggins
0-8163-1173-0. US$6.99, Cdn$10.49.

Tina, the Really Rascally Red Fox
VeraLee Wiggins
0-8163-1321-0. US$6.99, Cdn$10.49.

Skeeter, the Wildly Wacky Raccoon
VeraLee Wiggins
0-8163-1388-1. US$6.99, Cdn$10.49.

Lucy, the Curiously Comical Cow
Corinne Vanderwerff
0-8163-1582-5. US$5.99, Cdn$8.99.

Thor, the Thunder Cat
VeraLee Wiggins
0-8163-1703-8. US$6.99, Cdn$10.49.

Prince, the Persnickety Pony
Heather Grovet
0-8163-1787-9. US$6.99, Cdn$10.49.

Prince Prances Again
Heather Grovet
0-8163-1807-7. US$6.99, Cdn$10.49.

Petunia, the Ugly Pug
Heather Grovet
0-8163-1871-9. US$6.99, Cdn$10.49

Nibbles the Mostly Mischievous Monkey
Martha Myers
0-8163-1947-2. US$6.99, Cdn$10.49.

Order from your ABC by calling **1-800-765-6955**,
or get online and shop our virtual store at
www.adventistbookcenter.com.

- Read a chapter from your favorite book.
- Order online.
- Sign up for email notices on new products.